Lessons & Leather

A steamy, small-town opposites-attract romance between a woman learning to want and a man learning he's wanted.

Hana York

Pink Pop Publishing

Lessons & Leather

(The Thorne Sisters Book 4)

www.HanaYork.com

Contents

Prologue 1

1. Chapter One 5
2. Chapter Two 16
3. Chapter Three 26
4. Chapter Four 35
5. Chapter Five 47
6. Chapter Six 54
7. Chapter Seven 61
8. Chapter Eight 71
9. Chapter Nine 76
10. Epilogue 83
11. Hana York Books 95

12. About the Author 97

13. More to Read 99

Prologue

ELIZA

The school parking lot was quiet when I pulled in—just a few scattered cars and the faint smell of mulch from the new flower beds.

I didn't turn off the engine right away.

Instead, I sat briefly, hands wrapped around my travel mug, steam curling against the windshield like a quiet reminder: you're okay. You're ready.

A tray of cupcakes wobbled in the passenger seat every time I breathed too hard. Twenty-four pink-frosted sugar bombs, each topped with a cherry gummy. A thank-you for the janitor. A pick-me-up for the front office. A treat for the kindergartners who spelled "hippopotamus" correctly yesterday, which was more than I could manage without spellcheck.

I nudged the tray toward the center of the seat, next to my tote bag bursting with construction paper and glitter glue. The bag slumped sideways, spilling a handful of googly eyes into the cup holder.

Of course it did.

I smiled. This was my version of chaos—glue sticks, snack schedules, and a running tally of which child had most recently eaten a crayon.

The smile faded.

Because underneath the glitter, cherry earrings, and extra napkins, there was this hum of something I couldn't name. A weight I'd carried so long it felt like mine.

I was good at being the reliable one. The cheerful one. The one who made everything easier.

But some mornings, I wondered what it would feel like to rely on someone else.

Not because I couldn't do it alone, but because I was tired of always having to.

And I hated that thought.

Because my sisters were my safety net, whether I admitted it or not.

Lola fought for me when I couldn't find the words.

Vivian dared me to live louder, even when I wanted to hide.

And Veronica always seemed to know what I needed. Gave me truth instead of comfort and reason to laugh when I wanted to cry.

They loved me. I knew that.

But sometimes... I still felt like the footnote in my own story.

I shook it off. Adjusted the radio. Slipped the car into drive.

And bumped straight into the back of the largest truck I'd ever seen.

My breath caught.

The tray of cupcakes lurched.

Pink frosting smudged.

No. No, no, no—

Where the heck did that thing come from?

I threw the car into park, grabbed napkins, and tried to clean it up, smearing frosting and nerves in equal measure.

The truck door opened, and a man stepped out.

Tall. Broad. Wearing a plain gray tee stretched over shoulders that should've come with a warning label.

He glanced at the back of his truck. Then at my car. Then at me.

And I knew—with total certainty—I was about to cry in front of someone who looked like he hadn't cried about anything in his entire life.

Wonderful.

Absolutely wonderful.

Chapter One

CLAY

The hit wasn't hard. Just enough to rock the truck and slosh half my coffee into the center console.

This was precisely why I avoided the school lot; there were too many minivans and distractions, and everyone was trying to do six things at once before eight a.m.

I exhaled through my nose. Counted to five.

Then I opened the door.

The car behind me was small. Pale blue. The front bumper barely nudged into mine like it regretted the decision halfway through.

Inside, the driver sat frozen.

Brown curls piled on top of her head in a loose bun. Big eyes, flushed cheeks, and a look of pure panic behind the windshield. I'd seen that face once or twice at pick-up—Miss Thorne. Kindergarten teacher.

She looked horrified. Like she'd taken out my entire back end instead of tapping it at less than two miles an hour.

She stared at the steering wheel, as if hoping it might explain how this happened.

Then her gaze flicked to mine, and her whole face crumpled.

She climbed out slowly, eyes wide, hands fluttering like she wasn't sure what to do with them.

"I'm so sorry," she said, wringing her hands. "I looked down for one second to check on the cupcakes, and then there was a glitter spill. And now I'm here. In your truck."

She winced. "Not in your truck. Into. I bumped into your truck. Oh my god."

I said nothing.

Mostly because I didn't trust my mouth not to do something stupid.

Like smile.

She stepped closer, scanning the back of the truck like it might burst into flames at any second.

"Is it... bad? I don't see a dent. But that doesn't mean there isn't one. I mean, sometimes there's structural damage you can't see, right?"

She turned to me—earnest, hopeful, doomed.

I glanced at the bumper. Wiped my thumb along the edge where her license plate had tapped it.

"No damage."

"Oh. Thank god." She let out a breath, her hand pressing to her chest.

"I still feel awful." She glanced back at her car. "Can I offer you a cupcake? I brought extras."

Her voice wavered, like she wasn't sure if she was offering a treat or an apology.

"Vanilla with cherry buttercream. Some of them are a little—um, wonky. But they're still good."

There was glitter on her cheek. One lone sprinkle clinging to her blouse.

She winced. "Sorry. I ramble when I'm... well. This."

Her hand fluttered like she was trying to wave away the whole situation.

"I'm Eliza Thorne. I teach kindergarten here."

I nodded. "Clay Walker."

Her eyebrows lifted, waiting for more.

"Maggie's my niece. She's in your class."

Recognition bloomed fast. "Maggie! Of course. She's wonderful. So curious. She always asks the best questions."

"Yeah," I said. "That sounds like her."

Eliza smiled—soft and warm.

And something in my chest pulled tight.

I should've walked away.

Said "no damage." Got back in the truck.

But I didn't.

I just stood there like an idiot, watching her ramble about cupcakes with frosting on her fingers and glitter on her cheek.

I knew women like her. Sweet. Scattered. The kind who carried half the world on their shoulders and apologized when it got heavy.

Too bright. Too sweet. Too good for a man like me.

I knew what I looked like—big, broad, scruff on my jaw, grease under my nails. Ten years of mistakes and not a lot to show for them.

And around here, that's all people need. One glance and they think they've got me figured out.

Grumpy. Rough. Intimidating. Trouble if you're not careful.

They're not wrong.

And whatever this was—this pull?

It didn't matter.

Because women like her don't pick men like me.

And if they do, they don't stay.

She hesitated, then looked up at me with wide, hopeful eyes.

"I know there's no damage," she said, "but... can I still give you a cupcake?"

She tucked a curl behind her ear. "It would make me feel better."

And I should've said no.

I should've crossed my arms and done what people expected from someone like me.

But no one offered me cupcakes. Not without a smirk. Not without a joke about how I didn't look like the type who liked sweet things.

No one looked at me the way she did.

Like I wasn't a warning sign.

Like I was just... a man.

So I nodded. "Yeah. Sure."

Her whole face lit up—soft, like sunlight catching on glass.

She hurried back to the car, reached into the cupcake carrier, and carefully picked one. When she returned, she handed it to me like a peace offering. Or a promise.

"Still in one piece," she said. "Mostly."

I took it. Let my fingers brush hers, just for a second.

A spark. Small, stupid. Enough to short-circuit something in my chest.

"Thanks," I said gruffly. Like it was no big deal. Like it didn't matter.

But the way she looked at me? That was going to stay with me.

ELIZA

I tried to go about my day like I hadn't rear-ended the hottest man I'd ever seen.

Like he hadn't stepped out of that truck with broad shoulders, steady hands, and a voice that made *thanks* sound like a threat and a promise.

But I couldn't shake him.

Not through morning greetings, bulletin board prep, or even while answering an earnest question about whether dragons eat grilled cheese.

My thoughts kept circling back to him.

To the quiet way he watched me. The way his presence filled the space without taking it over.

To the impossible fact that a man like that—gruff, grounded, and built like a mountain—had looked at me like I wasn't just sweet. Like maybe I was something more.

And it was ridiculous.

I had twenty-four students, three parent emails to answer, and a glitter explosion still waiting in the supply closet. I did not have time for a crush.

The bell rang, and my classroom filled with tiny voices and oversized backpacks.

Greta was wearing her astronaut helmet again. Liam had already lost a shoe. Someone sneezed with the force of a cannon.

"Good morning, my brilliant beans," I said, clapping my hands. "Coats on hooks, bags in cubbies, then find your seat for morning meeting."

They shuffled into motion with the kind of semi-controlled chaos only kindergarten could produce.

I crouched to help Greta with her backpack zipper, and there it was again, that voice in my head.

Thanks.

Low. Rough. Just slightly surprised.

I stood too fast and bumped into the edge of my desk.

"Miss Thorne?"

Maggie Walker stood beside me, her backpack already hung, hands folded in front of her like the tiny old soul she was.

"Yes, Maggie?"

She tilted her head. "Are you okay? You look like you're thinking really hard."

I smiled. "Just a lot on my mind today."

She nodded. "Sometimes when I think too hard, I have to eat a snack."

Honestly? Not a bad plan.

"I'll keep that in mind. Thanks. Go find your spot on the rug."

She skipped away, and I took a deep breath, letting the hum of the classroom settle around me like armor.

***

By the time the last student had been picked up, the glitter spill contained, and my inbox mostly ignored, I was running on caffeine and cupcake fumes.

So, when Lola texted: *Thrift therapy? Meet us at The Lucky Rack?* I didn't hesitate.

Retail therapy with my sisters wasn't exactly relaxing, but it was comforting in its chaotic, opinion-heavy way.

And safer than going home and thinking about Clay Walker.

Lola was elbow-deep in a bin of vintage denim, muttering about someone ruining a perfectly good jacket with rhinestones. Vivian tried on oversized sunglasses in front of a cracked mirror, and Veronica was at the rack, fingers gliding over silk like she had all the time in the world.

I wandered toward the kitchenware section. There was something oddly comforting about mismatched mugs.

"You're quiet," Lola said without looking up. "That usually means you're overthinking something or planning to adopt a stray."

"Neither," I said. "Just... distracted."

Vivian raised an eyebrow. "By?"

I hesitated. "I may have... lightly rear-ended someone in the parking lot this morning."

All three of them looked up.

"Wait, what?" Veronica said. "Are you okay?"

"Fine. Barely a tap. No damage. He was very..." I searched for the right word: "understanding."

"Uh-huh," Vivian said slowly. "And?"

"And... hot."

That got their attention.

"Who was it?" Lola asked, instantly suspicious.

"Clay Walker," I said, trying to sound casual. Like it didn't matter. Like he hadn't been in my head all day.

Lola froze, her hand still tangled in denim. "Absolutely not."

I blinked. "What?"

She stood up, arms crossed. "He's too big. Too broody. Too rough. That man looks like he could break hearts just by breathing."

"That's dramatic," I said.

"It's accurate," she replied. "He doesn't do relationships—he does repairs, silence, and probably a lot of glaring."

Vivian adjusted her sunglasses. "He's... intense. Not uninteresting. But he might be too much for you."

I opened my mouth, but she held up a finger. "Not because you're fragile. But because you're kind. And men like him don't always know what to do with kindness."

Veronica leaned against a rack, one brow raised. "Or maybe kindness is exactly what he needs. And our sister's allowed to want a man who looks like he'd throw a wrench through a wall if someone hurt her."

Lola rolled her eyes. Vivian didn't argue.

Veronica looked at me. "You're allowed to want, Eliza. That's not a weakness."

I nodded. Quietly. Because I knew they meant well. I knew they loved me.

But how they said it—too rough, too intense, too much—felt familiar.

And for once, I didn't want to be the sweet one everyone worried would get hurt.

I wanted to be the kind of woman a man like Clay Walker couldn't look away from.

And for a moment this morning, I could almost believe I was.

Chapter Two

CLAY

Maple Hill Elementary smelled like sanitizer and fruit snacks.

Not exactly my comfort zone.

Too clean. Too bright. Too many memories of being told to sit still and quiet down.

But the school needed help. Budget cuts meant the janitor was covering too much, and someone had requested assistance with a broken swing and shelves in a kindergarten classroom.

I had time, I had tools, and I said yes a little too fast when they mentioned the room number.

12B.

Eliza's classroom.

I wasn't getting paid for this and didn't want to be.

Maggie was here. Eliza was here.

That was reason enough.

The secretary at the front handed me a note. "Everything you need should be in the supply closet."

I nodded and kept walking. Neat, rounded handwriting in purple ink.

Shelf in Room 12B. Swing on the east playground. Storage closet hinge. Thank you! – Eliza Thorne

I read it twice. Not because I didn't get it.

I shifted the weight of the toolbox and headed to her room.

Room 12B was supposed to be empty.

I'd timed it that way.

I figured the kids would be at lunch, and I could finish the shelves without getting in anyone's way.

But the second I stepped inside, I saw her.

Kneeling on the rug, hair slipping from her bun, fingers stained with green paint and glitter. Surrounded by paper scraps and kid-sized scissors.

And I felt that same low, steady pull I hadn't been able to shake since she rear-ended my truck and offered me a cupcake like it was a lifeline.

She looked up.

And I forgot why I was there.

"Mr. Walker?" she said, blinking like she wasn't sure I was real. Her eyes flicked to the toolbox, then back to my face. "Is everything okay?"

"Clay," I said. "Just Clay."

She straightened, smoothing her skirt with paint-streaked hands. "Okay... Clay."

"The office said the shelves in here needed fixing."

Her expression softened. "Oh—yes. That shelf's been threatening collapse for months. I wasn't expecting anyone today."

He shrugged. "There was a call for volunteers in the parent newsletter. My brother flagged it for me. Figured I had the tools. And the time."

Her brows lifted slightly. "You did?"

I nodded.

She smiled. And it did something dangerous to my resolve.

"Well... thank you. That's really kind of you."

I didn't know what to say, so I looked past her to a shelf leaning like it was too tired to stand straight.

"Shouldn't take long," I muttered.

"Want me to clear the area?" she asked, gathering glue sticks.

I shook my head. "You don't have to leave."

She paused. "Okay. I'll stay out of your way."

I didn't tell her I wouldn't mind the opposite.

I just knelt by the shelf and opened the toolbox, like I hadn't come here hoping to see her.

"I'm sorry the room's a mess," she said. "The kids are designing seed packets for the class garden. It's adorable in theory. In practice, it's chaotic."

I glanced at a piece of construction paper that said *SUNFLOWER* in bubble letters, surrounded by glittery stickers and what looked like a vampire carrot.

"Looks like they're having fun."

"They are," she said, her whole face lighting up. "They love having something that's theirs, you know?"

I didn't, not really. But I nodded anyway.

"I knew you had the garage," she said. "But I didn't realize you fixed school shelves on your day off."

The fact that she knew anything about me settled deep in my chest, like a touch I didn't see coming.

I didn't let it show. Just shrugged. "They needed fixing."

Her smile tugged at the corner of her mouth. "You always this generous with your time?"

"No."

It came out flatter than I meant, but she didn't backpedal or get flustered.

"Need help holding anything? Not that I'm implying you can't do it alone," she added quickly. "You just look like you could use a second pair of hands."

I nodded, trying not to sound as affected as I felt. "All right. Hold the left side up for me."

She stepped in close enough that I caught the soft scent of vanilla and something floral.

When she lifted the shelf, our arms brushed, a subtle contact that sent a jolt straight through me.

She didn't flinch, but her breath hitched—just slightly.

Something shifted between us, in the air, in me.

She looked up, wide-eyed, lips parted like she might say something.

But she didn't.

And neither did I.

I just tightened my grip on the drill, anchored the bracket, and tried to focus on the work, not the way one brush of her skin had completely undone me.

ELIZA

He was close enough to rattle me completely.

His arm brushed mine as he anchored the shelf, and I could feel the heat rolling off him, steady and warm like sunlight after a storm.

I wanted to lean into it.

Curl into him like a cat and stay there.

Which was... alarming.

I tried to focus on the task, but all I could think about was how solid and warm he felt.

And then there was the smell of him.

Not cologne—nothing artificial. Just clean skin, warm cotton, the faint scent of cedar, heat, and something dangerous.

It did strange things to my body.

Unexpected things.

My heart beat faster. My breath hitched.

I swallowed hard and risked a glance at his face.

Focused. Calm. Like this was just another shelf on just another Tuesday.

I wasn't calm. Not even close.

And the worst part?

I didn't want to be.

He secured the last screw, gave the shelf a quick shake, then straightened.

"Should hold now," he said.

I nodded. "Looks great. Thank you."

He gave a slight shrug. "You're welcome." His eyes swept the room—the art projects, the glitter, the barely contained chaos. "Maggie says your classroom is crazy—but the good kind."

He paused, then added, "Feels like you've figured out how to make the chaos feel safe."

The words settled deep, unexpected, and steady.

People noticed the bright bulletin boards. The tidy cubbies. The songs, stickers, and smiles.

But not the effort beneath it. Not the way I worked to keep the chaos from swallowing the gentle parts.

And the way he looked at me—steady, warm, like he meant it—

It made my knees feel a little loose.

I smiled because it was the only thing I could think to do. "You're not so bad at steadying things yourself."

His mouth curved, just barely. "Different kind of mess."

I meant to say something back. Something light. Maybe even clever.

But the way he looked at me—steady, quiet, almost reverent—stopped the words in my throat.

The room felt suddenly still. Like the air between us had gone quiet.

He didn't look away.

And neither did I.

His gaze flicked down, just once, to my mouth.

And then he leaned in. Just a little.

I didn't move. Couldn't.

My heart thudded in my chest, loud enough to drown out thought.

And then—

Laughter echoed from the hallway.

We jumped apart like someone had flipped on a light.

Clay stepped back quickly, toolbox in hand.

The moment folded up between us like it hadn't happened at all.

He cleared his throat.

"I'm headed out to the playground," he said. "To look at that swing on your list."

I cleared my throat. "I can show you the way. It's tucked around the side, near the cafeteria."

He nodded. "Sounds good."

Clay walked beside me, steps steady, shoulders broad enough to block the sun if he tried.

We rounded the corner to the east playground, and he scanned the structure like he was already cataloging what needed attention.

"The swing's over there," I said, pointing. "One of the chains keeps catching."

He nodded and headed toward it.

I lingered nearby, watching him work without really meaning to.

And that's when I saw Max.

Perched at the top of the monkey bars, frozen halfway across.

He wasn't in my class, but I knew that look—panic creeping in, too proud to call for help.

Before I could take a step, Clay was already moving.

He didn't shout or panic.

Just walked over, calm and sure, and stopped at the base of the structure.

"You okay up there?" he asked, voice low and steady.

Max didn't answer. Just held on tighter.

Clay didn't push. Didn't crowd him.

He stood still, hands loose at his sides.

"You're doing great," he said. "Take your time."

His voice dropped a little, softer now. "I've gotten stuck before, too."

That was all it took.

Max exhaled, scooted forward one bar at a time, and reached the platform.

Clay held out a hand. No pressure. No urgency.

Just there. Just steady.

And when Max took it, something in my chest squeezed tight.

Because yes, Clay Walker was big. Brooding. Looked like he could crush a wrench with one hand.

But I'd just watched him coax a scared kid down from the monkey bars without raising his voice or breaking a sweat.

And no matter what people in town said about him...

I knew better now.

Chapter Three

CLAY

The kid's hand was small in mine.

Sweaty. Shaky.

But he held on.

Didn't cry. Didn't panic. Just breathed through it—step by step—until he was back on solid ground.

"Nice work," I said quietly.

He nodded and took off toward the picnic tables as if nothing had happened.

I watched him go. Made sure his shoulders uncurled. His pace evened out.

When I turned, Eliza watched me with an admiration I wasn't sure I'd earned.

Like what I'd just done hadn't surprised her.

Like it had confirmed something she already believed.

That I was good.

And I couldn't remember the last time anyone had looked at me like that.

It hit harder than that almost-kiss in her classroom.

***

The swing wasn't complicated—just a kinked chain and a loose bolt. Fifteen minutes of easy work.

But I couldn't stop thinking about her. The way she hadn't flinched when I leaned in. The way she'd looked at me, like I was something steady. Something worth admiring.

I should've felt steady, too.

Instead, I drove back to the shop, my grip too tight on the wheel, and my thoughts too loud to ignore.

The garage was quiet when I got there.

Concrete floors. Humming lights. Tools right where I left them.

I used to like the stillness.

Today, it felt too empty.

I wiped down the bench. Checked the inventory clipboard.

Tried to shake her voice from the back of my mind.

Then came the telltale thud of boots against concrete.

Tanner.

He didn't knock. Just walked in, grabbed a root beer from the fridge, and leaned against the counter like this was a social call.

"Lola mentioned the fender bender," he said casually.

I wiped my hands on a rag. "She barely tapped my bumper."

"Right," he smirked. "And then gave you a cupcake."

I didn't answer.

He took a sip, watching me. "Just so we're clear—Lola's already sharpening knives. So if you're gonna mess around with Eliza..."

"I'm not."

He raised an eyebrow.

I didn't flinch. "I'm not."

Tanner leaned back, slow and easy. "Okay. Then what are you doing?"

I returned to wiping down the same wrench I'd already cleaned twice.

"She's... nice," I said finally. "Kind."

He laughed under his breath. "Yeah, Clay. She's also a grown woman. Not a rescue dog."

"She looked at me like I was... good," I muttered. "Like I wasn't someone to be avoided."

There was a pause before Tanner said, "Maybe that's because you are good."

I shook my head. "Not the kind of good she deserves."

"You let her decide that."

He finished the root beer and set the bottle down with a soft clink.

He turned to me with a look that was steady, serious. No trace of his usual grin.

"Look. I know what people in this town say about you. And I know that's all bullshit."

I didn't move.

"But Eliza?" His voice dropped. "She's not just Lola's sister. She's *Eliza*. You hurt her, even by accident, you're not just answering to me. You're answering to three very protective sisters. And trust me, they're a hell of a lot scarier than me, man."

He paused and then added, "So if you're in, be in. And if you're not... walk away now."

He didn't wait for an answer.

Just gave me one last look and walked out.

The garage door creaked shut behind him.

And the silence settled back in.

But for once, I didn't know what the hell to do with it.

ELIZA

I didn't mean to cry.

I told myself I just needed to grab more glue sticks.

But really, I needed a minute.

Just one quiet minute.

The supply closet was cool, cramped, and smelled like old paper and lemon cleaner. I sat on the floor beside a box of construction paper, blinking hard at the shelves, trying not to cry.

A parent had stopped me in the hall this afternoon.

"You're adorable," she'd said, with a smile that didn't quite reach her eyes. "The kids must think of you like a big sister. Hopefully, they'll have a *real* teacher next year to keep them on track."

The words clung to me like glitter. Light on the surface. Impossible to shake.

I'd smiled, like I always do. Nodded. Said thank you.

And then I hid in the supply closet.

I *was* young, sweet, smiley, and glittery.

But I was more than that.

I was also the kind of teacher who made up songs about handwashing and stayed up late cutting bulletin board flowers.

The kind who built lesson plans from scratch, met with parents after hours, read education journals, and worried about my students as if it were a second job.

And I was tired—bone-deep tired-of being treated like a Pinterest board in a cardigan.

The tears came faster now, no matter how hard I blinked.

So I curled in on myself, arms around my knees, and tried to ride it out.

Which, of course, was when the door opened.

I stiffened. Swiped at my cheeks.

"Sorry—just grabbing—" The voice stopped me cold.

"Miss Thorne?"

Clay.

Of course.

I scrambled to my feet too fast, knocking into a crate of dry erase markers. "Hi! Sorry—I was just..."

He stepped in, frowning gently. "They told me the hinge in here needed fixing. Didn't think anyone would be inside."

I stood quickly, brushing my skirt. "Sorry. I didn't mean to be in the way."

He glanced at the crate. The tissues in my hand. My blotchy face.

"You okay?"

I nodded. Then, I shook my head.

And the tears came all over again.

Clay didn't say anything.

He just stepped forward, calm and confident, and closed the door behind him.

Then, without asking, without hesitating, he wrapped his arms around me.

No questions. Just warm, solid comfort.

I froze for a beat. Then melted into him like I belonged there.

He held me like it was the easiest thing in the world.

And for the first time all day, I could breathe.

His chest was warm beneath my cheek, rising and falling in a rhythm that calmed me.

No one had ever held me like this before.

Like I wasn't a burden. Like I didn't have to apologize for needing this.

And somewhere between the weight of his arms and the quiet strength of his presence, the tears began to slow.

I breathed in slowly and deeply, and didn't pull away.

Instead, I whispered the only thing I could manage. "Thank you."

He didn't answer.

I leaned back to look at him, and that's when I saw it.

It wasn't just concern. Or kindness. There was something deeper in his eyes—something that looked a lot like want.

He didn't speak or move.

But the air between us shifted, electric and still.

I slid my hand to his chest, right over his heart. It was racing. So was mine.

And then he kissed me.

Not cautiously. Not like he was testing the moment.

Like he'd been carrying the want of it for miles and finally let it break free.

His mouth met mine with a heat that stole my breath, with a tenderness that made me ache.

His hand slid to the back of my neck, fingers threading into my hair, steady, sure, and a little bit reverent.

I curled into him, fists clutching the worn fabric of his shirt, like maybe if I held tight enough, I could keep this moment from slipping away.

The kiss was deep. Consuming. The kind you only get once—the kind that says, *You matter. You're wanted. You're real.*

And when he sighed into my mouth—low and rough, all unraveling control—I felt something inside me break open.

Not painfully.

But with relief.

Like this wasn't just a kiss.

It was a beginning.

And I would never forget it.

Chapter Four

CLAY

I'd kissed women before. Plenty.

But nothing like this.

This wasn't just heat or sweetness—it was trust.

The way she leaned into me, like I was something steady, something safe. Like she believed I could handle her trust, and wanted me to have it.

That's what undid me.

Not the softness of her lips or how her fingers curled into my shirt.

It was the way she gave me this moment, unguarded.

Like she didn't doubt for a second that I'd take care of it.

She sighed into my mouth, low and quiet, and I felt it everywhere. In my chest. My gut. My hands twitched at my sides, itching to pull her closer.

I wanted more.

More of that sound. More of her, wrapped around me like a secret I hadn't earned but couldn't let go of. More of the way she tilted her face like she already knew how I kissed and wanted every inch of it.

I could've lost myself right there—

Would've, if she'd made one more sound like that.

If she'd pulled me even a breath closer, I wouldn't have stopped.

But Eliza Thorne didn't deserve a rushed moment in a supply closet.

She wasn't a fleeting thing.

And I didn't want to be the kind of man who treated her like one.

So I pulled back, just enough to breathe.

She blinked up at me, kiss-drunk and flushed, and it nearly broke my resolve.

"I should go," I said, my voice rough around the edges.

Her hand was still on my chest.

Stepping back felt like tearing something essential from my skin.

"I'll fix the hinge next time." Then I turned and walked out.

Because if I stayed, I was going to forget where we were. Forget everything but her body against mine, and the way she came undone in my arms.

***

The beer sat on the counter, half-warm and untouched. I'd pulled it from the fridge over an hour ago, cracked it open, taken a sip, and never gone back. Now it just sat there, sweating.

The house was quiet. Too quiet.

No music. No engine hum. No Maggie asking if I could fix her scooter again. Just me, and the kiss I couldn't stop replaying.

Her lips. Her fingers curled in my shirt. That soft, impossible sigh.

I'd felt it everywhere. And now I couldn't get it out of my head.

I closed my eyes and tried to shake it, but it didn't work. I could still feel the weight of her pressed into me, the heat, the way she didn't pull away. The way she looked at me when I did.

Not angry. Not confused. Just... open. Like she trusted me to do the right thing.

And I had, maybe.

Because the truth was, I didn't know how to be what she needed. Not really.

She deserved someone steady. Someone who didn't stumble over his own silences or second-guess every word.

Someone who didn't carry ten years of silence in his bones.

I looked down at my hands—rough, calloused, scarred from a dozen engines and a thousand hours of work.

Hands that were good at fixing things.

But I didn't know if they were good at holding on.

Especially to someone like Eliza Thorne.

Someone who made the world softer.

Who made me want things I hadn't let myself want in a long time.

Didn't matter.

Because I already knew the truth.

I was falling.

And the only question now was whether I was brave enough to land.

I didn't know how to sit with this kind of wanting.

Didn't know what to do with the way my body felt coiled and hot.

I'd pulled back from her. Walked out. Done what I thought was right.

And now I was alone, with nothing but my own indecision.

I sighed. Turned off the kitchen light.

The bedroom wasn't much better—just a bed, a dresser, and a few shirts draped over the chair.

But it was dark. Quiet.

A little less like standing in the middle of a decision I didn't know how to make.

I sat on the edge of the bed. Rubbed a hand over the scruff on my jaw.

Then I lay back. Closed my eyes.

It was a losing battle.

Trying not to think about her.

That kiss.

She'd leaned in, soft and certain, like I was something good.

My breath hitched. My body tightened.

I thought about her mouth. Her small fingers tugging at my shirt. That sound she made—the low, sweet sigh that went straight to my gut.

I groaned out loud.

How the hell was I this desperate when I'd barely even touched her?

My hands trembled as I unfastened the button on my jeans. The zipper followed—loud in the quiet room.

I freed my cock, the cool air a jolt across flushed skin.

I was hard. So fucking hard.

I bit back a groan and wrapped my hand around the ache.

I stroked slowly at first, grip firm, the rhythm steady.

A bead of pre-cum slid from the tip. I used it, dragging my palm over the head.

My hips rocked, instinct driving the pace.

I thought about Eliza.

The curve of her neck.

The softness under my hands.

The way she'd look if I were inside her—wide-eyed and flushed, holding on tight.

My hand moved faster, grip tightening as I chased the high I could already feel building.

A strangled moan tore from my throat. I didn't try to stop it, my hips jerking as the tension coiled tight.

One more stroke. One more second and I came hard.

The release hit like a punch rolling through me in crashing waves.

I gasped, sweat beading along my spine.

And when it passed, when the last tremor faded, I knew one thing for sure.

This wasn't even close to what it would feel like with her.

But damn if I didn't want to find out.

ELIZA

After school, I headed straight to Pleasure & Co.

I needed to talk to Veronica.

And it needed to be in person.

She looked up as soon as I walked in, sharp eyes catching mine over the rim of a clipboard.

"That's a face," she said. "What happened?"

I hesitated near the counter, fingers curling in the hem of my cardigan.

"I kissed him," I said.

Veronica blinked. "Well. Okay then. Come on."

She guided me to the back room and poured two glasses of wine.

And just like that, I started talking.

"Clay's been helping out at the school," I said. "Fixing stuff. Shelves, playground equipment. I guess the office called in a favor, and he showed up."

Veronica gave me a knowing look. "Uh-huh."

I tucked a knee up on the velvet loveseat and stared at my wine glass.

"I was in the supply closet. A parent said something that really got to me—told me I was adorable. Said the kids probably think of me as a big sister. That maybe next year they'd get a *real* teacher to keep them on track."

Veronica's mouth tightened, but she didn't interrupt.

"I didn't cry in front of her. I smiled. Nodded. Said thanks." I let out a breath. "But the second I was alone, I broke."

Veronica leaned back, her expression softening.

"I thought I was alone," I said. "Then Clay came in—he was supposed to fix the door hinge, and he found me on the floor, trying to get it together."

I could still feel the weight of his arms.

"He didn't say anything. Just closed the door and held me."

Veronica's brows lifted slightly.

"I've never been held like that before. Like I was allowed to fall apart."

The tears that pricked now weren't from pain. They were from the memory of safety.

"And then I looked up at him... and he kissed me."

Veronica didn't say a word.

"It wasn't rushed. It wasn't soft, either. It was—God. It was everything. I felt it everywhere. But the second I leaned into it, he pulled back. Said he had to go."

I shook my head. "And I just... I don't know how to be what he wants. I want him to want me. I want him to look at me like he can't help it. But I don't know how to get there."

Veronica didn't rush to answer. She set her glass down and waited for my eyes to meet hers.

"Sweetheart," she said, "you don't need to figure out how to be wanted. You already are."

"I want to be myself," I said. "I just... I've never done this before. Not any of it. I'm a virgin."

Veronica didn't rush to speak. She set her glass down and met my gaze, steady as ever.

"You're the only one I've ever told," I added. "Not even the others know. I didn't want them to think I was some delicate little girl who needed to be protected. You've all lived and loved and made bold choices. And I've just... been safe."

She reached for my hand and held it.

"You don't need experience to be desirable," she said. "You need honesty. Presence. Trust. You already have those in spades. And if Clay Walker has half a brain in that broody, brawny head of his—he's already half in love with you and doesn't know what to do about it."

I let out a shaky laugh.

Veronica smiled and leaned back. "Let yourself want this. That's the boldest thing you can do."

I glanced over at her. "Can I ask you something?"

Veronica raised a brow. "Eliza, you can ask me anything."

"I know I want to be with him. Intimately. On some deep level, I know that." I hesitated. "But the truth is... I don't really know what that means. Not fully."

Veronica's expression softened. 'You don't have to know everything to know what you want.'

I nodded slowly, the words catching in my throat.

"I've never been with anyone. Not even close. I've never made out with someone. Never... taken care of things on my own." My face warmed, but I kept going. "I've never explored that side of myself at all."

I shook my head. "And it feels like there's this whole world I'm supposed to just know how to navigate. But I don't. I don't even know what I like. So how can I even think about being with someone else if I haven't figured out any of that?"

Veronica's expression softened—not with pity, but with something close to admiration.

"Eliza," she said gently, "you don't have to know everything. You just have to be willing to learn yourself. That's where it starts—not with anyone else. With you. What feels good. What feels right. What feels like you."

I let out a shaky breath.

She leaned forward, voice low and sure. "You don't need permission to explore that side of yourself—and you sure as hell don't need to be experienced to deserve intimacy."

Veronica stood, crossed the room, and opened a small cabinet near the back wall.

She didn't say anything at first. Just sifted through the shelves like she was choosing a bottle of wine or the right shade of lipstick.

She turned back with a small satin bag in her hand.

"This isn't about the toy," she said, placing it gently in my lap. "It's about the choice. About giving yourself permission to figure out what you like—what feels good, what feels true. This is just one way in."

My fingers curled around the bag.

It was soft. Light. A little intimidating.

But mostly it felt like possibility.

I looked up. "What if I mess it up?"

Veronica smiled. "Eliza. You can't mess up pleasure. You can only ignore it. And you've done that long enough."

Something loosened in my chest.

Maybe it was the weight of all the years I'd spent waiting.

Maybe it was the quiet realization that I no longer had to wait.

Chapter Five

ELIZA

When I got to my apartment, I locked the door and set the bag on the bed.

Then I changed out of my school clothes and pulled on something soft and loose.

No music. No distractions. Just the quiet. And me.

For the first time, I didn't feel like I was waiting. I was present—in my body, in my choice, in the quiet pull of something I was finally ready to want.

I was nervous, but I lay back on my bed and let my fingers trail over my skin.

Tentative at first, I touched myself in a way I never had. My hands skimmed upward, teasing the curve of my breasts through the fabric, and I gasped when I brushed a nipple. The sensation lit me up, a delicious shiver running through me. I did it again—circling, pressing—feeling my nipples harden under my touch. I pinched one lightly and moaned, the sound foreign and wholly mine.

My body responded instantly. A rush of wet heat pooled low between my legs, making me ache in a way that felt both raw and thrilling. I'd never known this kind of pleasure. This kind of wonder.

I thought of Clay. His hands. His mouth. The way he kissed me like I was something sacred. Everything inside me tightened.

My breath quickened, and my fingers moved with more urgency. I squeezed and pinched, chasing the sweet, pulsing heat that had bloomed in my belly.

The ache between my legs was intense now, my panties damp, the fabric clinging to my swollen flesh. I arched off the bed, thighs pressing together.

My hand trembled as I reached for the toy, the satin bag sending a thrill up my spine. I opened it, breathless.

A clit simulator.

I slipped off my panties and settled back against the pillows. The cool air kissed my bare skin, making me shiver.

I held the toy in my hand. Read the instructions twice. Then pressed it to my clit and turned it on.

The first hum made me gasp, low and desperate.

The vibration was intense. I dialed it back, easing in. My hips lifted instinctively as I adjusted the setting, finding a rhythm that matched my racing heart.

I moaned, wet and throbbing, my body moving with the toy's pulse.

I pictured Clay. His hands on my hips. His mouth at my throat. His eyes dark with want.

A fresh wave of heat tore through me.

My thighs trembled. I tilted my hips with each thrust, the friction exact and perfect. The pleasure burned low and deep, coiling tighter.

I came with a cry, loud and breathless.

The orgasm ripped through me—hot, consuming, endless. Wave after wave crashed over me, each pulse stronger than the last.

I gasped, body trembling, the aftershocks leaving me raw and aching in the best way.

I hadn't known I could feel like this. So free. So full.

I lay there, breathless. Limbs heavy. Skin flushed.

I didn't feel new. Or changed. Just... more.

More present. More in tune with myself.

I'd touched something quiet and private—and now I wanted more.

More curiosity. More pleasure.

More of the spark Clay had stirred awake in me.

And I didn't want to wait.

CLAY

It was just past six when I locked up the front bay.

The air was cooling, but the place smelled like heat and engine grease.

I'd wiped down the tools, swept the floor, and told myself to head home.

But I didn't move.

I was still at the counter when the bell over the door chimed.

Probably forgot to lock up. Probably someone needing a jump.

But when I turned—it was Eliza.

She stood just inside the door, one hand hooked around the strap of her bag. Her hair was pinned up, wisps catching the light, and she wore a sweater the color of sun-warmed honey. Her expression was soft, steady, like she'd made up her mind and wasn't backing down.

My pulse hit like a misfired spark.

"I hope I'm not interrupting," she said.

"You're not." My voice came out rougher than I meant.

She stepped forward. Not shy. Not rushed. Just sure.

"I thought about waiting," she said. "But then I realized I didn't want to."

I stared.

"I've been doing that most of my life—waiting. To be ready. To be wanted. To feel like enough." Her eyes locked on mine. "But I'm not waiting anymore."

I swallowed hard.

"Eliza..."

She smiled—half bold, half uncertain. "You keep looking at me like I'm made of glass. I'm not."

I didn't move.

She came closer. Close enough that I felt that pull again.

"I'm not asking for perfect," she whispered. "I'm asking for real. For you."

I'd spent years keeping people at arm's length, thinking I was doing them a favor. But she didn't want space. She wanted me. And just like that, every excuse I'd clung to fell apart.

She stepped in further, looking at me like she already knew.

So I reached for her.

My hands settled at her waist, hesitant for half a second—until she leaned in, soft and certain—and then I was done.

I kissed her.

Not carefully or with caution, but with want.

With everything I hadn't let myself say.

Her hands slid under my shirt, fingers brushing skin, and she sighed against my mouth—soft, low, a sound that lit every nerve I had.

I backed her toward the counter, one slow step at a time, until her lower back met the edge of the wood.

She didn't pull away. Didn't hesitate or second-guess. She was here, choosing me, and I had never wanted anything more.

I kissed down her neck, lingering at the soft spot below her ear. She shivered under my touch, her hands fisting in my shirt, pulling me closer.

"Come here," I muttered against her skin, pulling back just enough to look into her eyes.

She nodded. Breathless. Ready.

I took her hand, led her through the side door, and into the office.

I pushed aside a stack of invoices, lifted her onto the desk, and slipped my hands beneath her sweater.

Her skin was soft and warm.

When I brushed my thumb over her nipple, she arched into me, a soft moan spilling from her lips.

I kissed her hard.

"Eliza." My voice was rough. "I want to taste you. Is that alright?"

Her breath hitched. "Yes. God, yes."

I kissed my way down her body—slow and sure—savoring the heat of her skin. Her ribs. Her stomach. The delicate curve of her hip.

Her head tipped back, lips parted, another needy sound escaping her that went straight to my cock.

I hooked my fingers under her panties and slid them down. Her breath shuddered out, quick, eager.

She was bare before me.

The most beautiful thing I'd ever seen.

I knelt, lifted one of her legs over my shoulder, and took in the sight before me.

Chapter Six

CLAY

Her scent hit me first—musky and sweet. I groaned, the sound vibrating against her skin. She was slick with want, and the first taste of her sent a jolt through my whole body.

Fuck. She was perfect.

Better than anything I'd ever imagined. I licked and sucked, slow at first, then faster as her hips bucked and her fingers tangled in my hair.

Her breath came fast, her thighs trembling against my shoulders.

My cock throbbed, painfully hard, but I didn't stop.

Wouldn't.

I wanted her to fall apart. Wanted to be the one who made it happen.

Her grip on my hair tightened. "Clay," she gasped—half plea, half demand. "More. I need more."

I slid a finger inside her, slow and careful.

Christ. She was tight.

She clenched around me, and I bit back a groan. Her body yielded, opening, until I felt it—her barrier.

Shock punched through me.

She was a virgin.

I almost stopped, but then she whimpered, her legs tightening, and I couldn't leave her hanging—not when she was so close.

I eased my finger back in, and she arched, moaning her pleasure.

I added another finger, stretching her gently, working her open and continued to lick her clit. It was swollen and throbbing, and I knew she was close, so close.

Her hips bucked against my mouth, the desk creaking beneath her. I fucked her with my fingers, careful not to breach that which I didn't have permission to take.

I could feel her climbing as her pussy tightened even more around my fingers.

And all I could think about was what it would feel like to sink into her. To be her first.

My hips rocked, instinctive, driven by the thought.

But I held myself back.

Because I wanted her to come. To feel the pleasure I could bring her.

"Clay," she cried. "I—" Her words broke.

I sucked her clit harder, fingers driving steady and sure and she shattered.

Her body arched off the desk, her cry sharp, sweet, and endless. I didn't stop. Stayed with her, fingers deep, mouth still moving, catching every aftershock, every pulse.

She slumped, breathless and glowing.

The most beautiful thing I'd ever seen.

I rose, gathered her into my arms. Her skin burned against mine, her chest rising and falling in a shaky rhythm.

I kissed her. She melted into it, soft and sweet.

Her arms wrapped around my neck. Fingers in my hair.

And I knew there was no coming back from this.

ELIZA

I couldn't breathe. Couldn't think. Couldn't believe how hard I'd just come.

The toy had been amazing—a revelation—but this?

This was ten thousand times better.

Clay's mouth, his hands, his everything had undone me, and I wasn't sure I'd ever be put back together.

I thought I knew what it meant to want, to feel, to be alive in my body.

Now, I realized I knew nothing.

Nothing but how impossibly good this was.

A stunned laugh bubbled out of me. I reached for him, needing to know he was real.

I kissed him and tasted myself on his tongue. Clay groaned low in his throat, cupped my face with both hands, and deepened the kiss. He kissed like he couldn't get enough, and my whole body responded—hungry for more.

"Clay," I whispered, breathless. "I can't believe how..." I flushed, heat blooming at the memory. "I didn't know it could feel like that."

His mouth curved into a wicked grin. "And that was just my mouth."

Heat pooled low in my belly again, want coiling tight.

"I want more," I said, meaning every word. "I want you."

I pulled him closer, fingers curled in his shirt.

Clay's hands stilled, eyes searching mine. Hesitant. Uncertain.

"You're a virgin," he said—not a question, not an accusation.

"Does that disappoint you?" My voice came out small, unsure.

He blinked. "What? No. Fuck, no." His hands rose to cradle my face, gentle and reverent. "Christ, Eliza. That just makes me want to earn every part of this. Every part of you."

My heart swelled—relief, desire, maybe even hope.

He didn't pull away. Didn't stop looking at me like I was the best thing that had ever happened to him.

"More than anything," he said, voice low and steady, "I want to be the one you trust with that. I want to be with you. More than I've ever wanted anything."

His breath was warm against my skin. "But not here. Not in the office. Not when I'm this close to losing my head."

I blinked, trying to follow.

He leaned in and kissed me again; this time, it felt like a promise.

"I want your first time to be somewhere special," he murmured, voice rough. "Not on my desk."

The warmth in my chest flickered and cooled. "So... you don't want to?"

He pulled back, the loss of contact like a slap of cold air.

"No," he said. "I mean—yes. I mean—"

My heart dropped.

He let out a ragged breath. "Eliza, I want you so fucking bad. That's why I'm trying to—"

But the doubt was already there. Burrowed deep.

I didn't hear the rest—not really. Because by then, I already knew where this was going.

He was pulling back again. Hesitating.

And I couldn't stand still and wait for it this time.

I slid off the desk, gathering the scattered pieces of myself—my shirt, my composure, the sting of wanting something I wasn't sure I was allowed to have.

"Thanks for... this," I said, my voice quiet as I crossed to the door. "I should go."

I didn't look at him. I didn't trust myself to.

Because the truth was already sinking in—too heavy, too familiar.

I was too much and not enough, all at once.

And he couldn't even say it.

Not clearly. Not without flinching.

My hand found the doorknob. I took a breath, steadying myself.

"See you around, Clay."

"Fuck," he said. "Eliza, wait—"

But I didn't.

I turned the knob, kept my head down, and walked out before he could see me cry.

I cursed my own stupidity as I drove home.

What had I expected?

That he'd be so overwhelmed with desire he'd take me right there, on his desk?

That he'd lose all control? That he'd want me so much he couldn't stop?

Maybe. Maybe that's precisely what I'd expected.

And maybe... I was more naive than I thought.

Chapter Seven

CLAY

I had to go after her before I lost my mind. Before she lost faith in me completely.

Because Eliza had it all wrong, and I needed to prove it.

The desk was still a mess. Her cardigan was on the floor. My hands were shaking.

I could still taste her on my tongue.

"Fuck," I muttered, staring at the empty doorway like it might spit her back out if I stood there long enough.

She thought I didn't want her.

Thought I was hesitating because of her.

Not because I wanted her so much, I could barely think.

I hadn't meant to hurt her. Jesus, I'd been trying to protect her. To make it right.

And I still managed to fuck it up.

I didn't even realize I'd pulled out my phone until it was already ringing.

Tanner picked up on the second ring. "Hey, man—"

"I need your help."

"What's going on? You okay?"

"No." I let out a breath. "I screwed up."

"What happened?"

"I said the wrong thing. Or maybe the right thing, but in the wrong way. She left. And I need to find her. But I don't know where she lives."

Another pause. Longer.

"You're talking about Eliza."

"Yeah."

He hesitated. "You hurt her?"

I gritted my teeth. "Not on purpose. But yeah. I think I did."

A sigh. "Clay—Lola's gonna skin you."

"I know. I don't care. Just tell me where she is so I can fix it."

Tanner was quiet for another moment.

"You better mean that."

"I do." My voice came out low. Honest. "She's the best thing that's ever happened to me. I'm not letting her walk away thinking I didn't want her."

Another beat.

Then Tanner gave me the address.

"Good luck," he said.

I was gonna need it.

I didn't wait to change. Just grabbed my keys, locked up, and got on my motorcycle.

The whole drive there, my mind spun.

What if she didn't open the door?

What if she didn't believe me?

I'd never chased anyone before.

Didn't know how to say the right thing, or how to fix something I broke with words instead of tools.

But I knew this, I wasn't letting her go without a fight.

When I pulled up to the address, the lights were on in the upstairs apartment.

I took the steps two at a time and knocked.

Nothing.

Knocked again. Firmer this time. "Eliza?"

Still nothing.

My chest tightened. I rubbed a hand down the back of my neck, about to knock again, when the door finally opened.

She stood barefoot, a soft cardigan over a tank top, her hair down, like she'd pulled it loose in frustration. Or exhaustion.

Her eyes were red like she'd been crying.

"Eliza," I breathed. "I'm sorry."

She didn't move at first.

"I need to explain," I said, my voice rough. "Just give me a minute. That's all I'm asking."

Still silent, she didn't slam the door—or speak. Instead, she opened it wider and stepped back.

I followed her inside, the air thick between us.

And right then, I made myself a promise: I was going to say every goddamn thing I should've said before she walked away.

I could've started with *I didn't mean it like that* or *You've got it all wrong.*

But that would've just been armor.

And I didn't want armor anymore.

Not with her.

So I said the only thing that mattered.

"I want you."

That got her eyes on mine.

"I want you so much it scares the hell out of me." I stepped closer. "And not because you're fragile. It's because you're real, and kind, and generous, and sexy as hell. And because you look at me like I'm more than the worst things people think about me."

Her mouth parted slightly, but she didn't interrupt.

"I'm not good at this," I said. "Saying the right thing. Doing the right thing. Growing up, there wasn't a lot of talking. No softness. No trust. You kept your head down and tried not to get in the way."

I scrubbed a hand through my hair.

"And I started believing I was the kind of man people tolerate. Not the kind they choose. But you make me feel like the man I've been trying to be was in there all along. Like maybe I just needed someone to see him."

I swallowed hard.

"I pulled back because I didn't want to mess it up. Because it meant something. *You* mean something. And I didn't want your first time to be a regret you carry."

Her expression shifted—something between hope and hesitation.

"I didn't pull back because I didn't want you." My voice dropped. "I pulled back because I want you too much."

I stepped closer, slow and steady.

"And if you still want me after this... I swear, I'm not going anywhere."

ELIZA

I uncrossed my arms. Stepped forward. Slowly.

I thought you were pulling away because you didn't want me." I said quietly.

His brow furrowed. "Eliza—"

"I know. That's not what you said." I looked up at him. "It's just... I've spent a long time feeling like I'm too much in all the wrong ways. Or not enough in the ways that count. And when you hesitated, even for a second... I heard every fear I've ever had."

His jaw tightened—not in anger, but in understanding.

"I thought you were rejecting me," I said, softer now. "And I ran before you could."

His chest rose, like he was holding something in. Maybe guilt. Maybe relief. Maybe both.

"I get why you wanted to slow things down," I said. "I just... needed to know you still wanted me."

"I do," he said, without hesitation. "I never stopped."

I reached out, brushing my fingers over the front of his shirt, slow and sure.

"Then stay."

My voice was so quiet I almost couldn't hear it over my heartbeat. "Please, Clay. Stay with me tonight."

I kissed him, soft at first, then full of all the longing I'd held back. He groaned into my mouth, a raw, rough sound that sent a thrill through me. His hands found my waist, pulling me close, grounding me, showing me this was real.

He backed me toward the bedroom, our bodies moving in a clumsy, hungry dance, neither of us willing to break the kiss until the backs of my knees hit the bed.

We went down together, his weight and warmth pressing into me. A soft moan escaped when I felt the full length of his cock hard against my thigh.

He caught himself on his elbows, his breath hot against my cheek. "Are you sure?" he asked, voice low, eyes locked on mine.

A wild, reckless joy bloomed in my chest.

"Oh my god, yes," I breathed. "I've never been more sure of anything."

Clay let out a shaky exhale. Then he kissed me again—deep and desperate—as his hands slid beneath my cardigan, pushing it off my shoulders before tugging my tank top up and over my head.

The cool air hit my skin, and I shivered, arching into him as he cupped my breasts, kneading them through the thin lace of my bra. My nipples tightened under his thumbs, and he groaned, his mouth finding mine again as I gasped.

Then he moved lower, his mouth replacing his hands. He sucked gently through the lace, his teeth grazing the peaks, and I moaned—a high, breathless sound.

"Please," I whispered, pulling him up to meet my eyes. "I want to feel you. All of you."

He reached behind me, unhooked my bra, and tossed it aside.

My body arched toward him, desperate and aching.

He growled low, the sound raw and full of promise, then lowered his mouth to my breast, sucking me into a wet, hot heat that shattered my breath.

My fingers threaded through his hair.

"Yes," I gasped as he moved to the other side, teasing the hardened peak with his tongue and teeth.

"Clay—yes."

The sensation was exquisite. Almost too much. A rush of need pooled between my legs, urgent and hot.

I tugged at his shirt, desperate to feel his skin against mine. He sat back, pulling it off in one smooth motion, and my hands flew to him, over the broad expanse of chest and muscle, memorizing him.

He was beautiful. Mine.

His eyes met mine, dark and molten. Then he lowered himself back over me, the thick length of him pressing hot and hard against my core, making my whole body come alive.

I wound my arms around his neck, hips rocking up against him, legs wrapping around his waist.

I could feel him—hard and insistent—and I wanted him inside me. Stretching. Filling. Claiming.

My fingers fumbled at the button of his jeans, trembling with need. With hunger. With the wild certainty that this was it. That *he* was it.

Clay's breath caught. He drew back slightly, his voice rough with restraint.

"Eliza, I'm big. And you're a virgin. I don't want to hurt you."

I blinked, heart skipping. "What?"

His face was tight, careful. "You're so small. And I'm... not. I need to get you ready first."

Relief and desire slammed through me, flooding every part of me.

He wasn't pulling away. He was protecting me.

"Clay, what if you don't..." My voice dropped. "What if you don't fit?"

The words barely made it out. I felt ridiculous saying them, but the fear was real. I'd never done this before.

His eyes darkened, and he made a low, guttural sound that sent heat spiraling through me.

He cupped my cheek, his voice low and steady.

"We'll make it work," he said. "I want this to be good for you, Eliza. I want it to be perfect."

Chapter Eight

CLAY

I kissed her again, slow and deep, letting her feel everything—my want, my certainty, my promise to take my time. I wasn't going to rush. I wasn't going to hurt her. I was going to make sure she was ready for me. Every inch of her.

I wanted her wet and wanting. I wanted to push her to the edge and hold her there until she was begging—so desperate for my cock she wouldn't notice the pain.

My hand slid down her body, pushing her shorts and panties down before I slipped a finger inside her. Christ, she was tight. Wet. Perfect. I moaned, my cock aching as I added another finger, stretching her gently. Her body tensed and fluttered around me, and I fought to keep my control. I kept my fingers buried deep and circled her clit with my thumb, coaxing her open, listening to the breathless sounds she made.

Her hips jerked into my hand, and she started to come apart, her moans turning frantic.

I wanted to feel her come again. I needed her relaxed, melted, ready to take me.

My pace quickened—deeper, harder—until she shattered, her body arching and clenching around my fingers. The hot, tight squeeze nearly undid me.

I waited until she was soft and pliant before pulling free, fumbling with my jeans, too far gone to slow down now. I kicked them off, my cock springing free, painfully hard. Her eyes widened.

"Clay," she whispered. "You're... big."

I let out a rough laugh. "I'll be gentle," I promised, settling between her legs.

I grabbed the condom from my back pocket, tore it open, and rolled it on with shaking hands. I was so fucking ready. So desperate to make her mine.

"Okay?" I asked.

She nodded, breathless.

I pressed the head of my cock to her slick pussy and eased in, just the tip, just enough to feel her heat.

I nearly lost it.

"Oh my god," she breathed.

I froze, straining to hold still.

"Okay?" I asked again.

"It's... a lot," she whispered.

"We can stop."

"No," she said quickly. "I want this. I want you."

I groaned, pushing in deeper, feeling her stretch around me, tight and hot and so goddamn perfect. Inch by inch, I filled her, holding back everything in me that wanted to move.

She pulsed around me, and I held still, letting her adjust.

"Fuck, Eliza," I whispered. "You're amazing."

Her hands gripped my back, her body trembling, but not pulling away. Her hips lifted, urging me deeper, and I lost a little more control.

Still, I went slow. Careful. Watching her.

And then—

"Clay, I'm not glass. I won't break." Her voice was thick with need. "Fuck me. Now. I need all of you."

I let out a groan that bordered on a growl, every muscle in me coiled and ready to snap.

I brought my thumb to her clit, circling softly, waiting for that final shift in her body. The moment she fully let go.

And then I pulled back and drove into her, breaking through her barrier with one deep thrust.

She gasped—a sharp intake of breath—but then, "Yes, Clay. Yes."

Her legs locked around me, her hips rising to meet mine. "Don't stop."

She was slick and hot and unbelievably tight. I thrust again, watching her face, reading every breath, every twitch, until I knew she was okay.

And then I gave in to it.

The rhythm built—hard, fast, the bed creaking beneath us. Her moans, her gasps, her body wrapped around min e... it was everything.

"Clay, I—" She didn't finish. Just arched, her body going taut as she came, her pussy clenching around me, pulling me with her.

I came hard, shuddering, my hips jerking as the pleasure tore through me. It was like nothing I'd ever felt—hot, raw, consuming.

I stayed inside her, holding her close, letting our bodies unwind together. Her chest pressed to mine, her breath soft against my neck.

I didn't move. Didn't want to.

Eliza was mine.

I didn't know if I believed in love. But if this wasn't it... I didn't know what else could be.

I rolled us gently, keeping her close. My skin was damp, my heart still racing.

She made a slight, sleepy sound and burrowed into me.

Fuck, she was perfect.

And I was the luckiest man alive.

I knew it wouldn't be easy. I'd screw up again. I'd have to prove myself to her, to everyone who thought I wasn't good enough.

But right now, none of that mattered.

Not the town. Not the past.

Just her.

"Eliza," I whispered, holding her tighter. "I'm not going anywhere. I'm not—"

But she was already asleep.

Already safe.

Already mine.

Chapter Nine

ELIZA

I woke to loud, insistent banging on the door. My body was still loose and tender, barely wrapped in the sheet. Clay was beside me, warm and solid, his arm draped over my waist.

"Someone's here," I murmured, still half-asleep.

He groaned, low and lazy. "Ignore it."

The knocking came again, louder this time.

"Maybe it's important?" I whispered.

Clay sighed and rolled out of bed, tugging on his jeans but skipping the shirt. He ran a hand through his hair, then gave me a long, lingering look like he was seriously considering climbing back in.

"I'll get it," he said.

I watched him walk away—barefoot, bare-chested, every muscle shifting under his skin. He opened the door, blocking the view with his body.

And then I heard the voice.

Familiar. Annoyed.

"Holy shit, Clay Walker."

Lola.

Panic surged. I scrambled for clothes, yanking on a tank top and panties, then grabbed the sheet and wrapped it around me like a toga, as if that might help.

I rounded the corner just in time to see Lola storm past Clay like a woman on a mission.

A very loud, very terrifying mission.

"I swear to God," she snapped, eyes blazing, "if you so much as messed up one hair on her head, I'll cut your brake lines and sleep like a baby."

Tanner followed, looking marginally apologetic. "I told her it might not be necessary—"

"You told me he hurt her," Lola hissed, spinning on him.

"Inadvertently!" Tanner shot back. "That's what he said. He inadvertently hurt her."

Lola turned back to Clay, who stood tall in my doorway, jaw tight, hands relaxed.

"Lola," I said, stepping into view, the sheet clutched around me like I was auditioning for a low-budget film.

Three heads swiveled toward me.

Clay's expression softened.

Lola's narrowed. "Are you kidding me right now?"

"I'm fine," I said quickly. "Everything's fine."

She looked between us, and my cheeks flushed.

"Oh my God," she muttered. "You're glowing. You're literally glowing." Her voice pitched into something between horror and awe. "I'm going to kill him and then bleach my eyeballs."

"Lola," Tanner said gently, "maybe we should—"

"I told you," she snapped. "Big. Broody. Trouble."

"I'm not trouble," Clay said, calm but firm. "And I'm not going to let you talk about me like I'm not standing here."

That stopped her.

"I care about your sister. I fucked up—yeah. But I fixed it. Or I'm trying to. And I'm not walking away."

Lola opened her mouth. Then closed it.

I stepped in. “I appreciate the concern. I do. But I’m okay. Clay didn’t hurt me.”

She turned to me, arms crossed. “Then why did Tanner say—”

“Because I freaked out,” I admitted. “I got scared. Misread something. Clay came after me. He explained. And now… we’re here.”

Lola stared. Then sighed and brushed invisible lint from her jacket.

“Well,” she said. “If you hurt her again, I’m not kidding about the brake lines.”

Clay nodded. “Understood.”

Tanner looked at both of us. “I need a drink.”

They didn’t stay long. Tanner managed to herd Lola out the door with a muttered, “Let’s go before she actually follows through on the bleach thing.”

Lola glared over her shoulder. “This isn’t over.”

Then they were gone.

The apartment was quiet again.

Too quiet.

I turned slowly, still swaddled in the sheet, and found Clay watching me.

Not guilty. Not cautious.

Just… watching.

"Sorry about that," I said, exhaling. "My sisters are very... invested."

He raised an eyebrow. "That was invested?"

I blinked.

He shrugged. "I was expecting weapons."

A surprised laugh bubbled out of me, breaking the tension.

He stepped forward and tucked a piece of hair behind my ear, his thumb grazing my cheek.

"You okay?" he asked.

I nodded. "Yeah. I think so."

His gaze held mine.

Then, just barely, he smiled. "Glowing, huh?"

I rolled my eyes. "Shut up."

"Make me," he murmured, and his mouth found mine.

His hands slipped under the sheet, pulling me in, the world falling away as he kissed me deeper. I tugged him toward the bedroom, not holding anything back.

He kicked off his jeans, and we tumbled into the bed—a tangle of limbs, laughter, and raw, desperate need. I straddled him, thighs braced on either side of his hips, hands flat against his chest.

For the first time, I felt in control.

His cock was hard beneath me, thick and hot, and I ground against him, both of us groaning at the contact.

He reached between us, his fingers teasing my clit, driving me wild.

"Clay," I gasped, hips rocking.

The pressure built fast, sweet, and electric.

I reached down, wrapping my hand around him, stroking slow and sure. He jerked into my grip, groaning.

"Clay," I panted. "Do you have another condom?"

His eyes darkened. "Fuck, yes. In my pants."

I reached down and grabbed one, handing it to him. He tore it open with shaking hands and rolled it on quickly.

Then Clay sat up, pulling me close, his mouth hot on my breast. I gasped, arching into him, guiding his cock to my entrance.

"Are you ready for this, sweetheart?" he asked.

"Yes," I breathed. "I'm ready."

I sank down onto him slowly, gasping as he stretched and filled me. So deep. So full. It was almost too much. And exactly right.

I rocked my hips, the pressure exquisite. He groaned, his hands tight on my waist. "Fuck, Eliza. Take me. Take it all."

I did.

I took everything. And it was glorious.

He sucked one nipple into his mouth, his fingers pinching and teasing the other, and I was gone—wild and wet and clenching around him.

I reached between us, stroked my clit, desperate and bold.

"Fuck, Eliza," he growled. "That's the sexiest thing I've ever seen. Take it, baby. Take your pleasure."

He thrust up into me, deep and hard.

"I want to watch you come."

His words undid me.

I stroked my clit faster, desperate, frantic, and rode him hard, slamming down on his cock as he rose up to meet me.

The orgasm hit hard. Sudden and blinding. My body trembled, clenching around him, my cry loud and raw.

Clay cursed and followed, his release crashing into mine, his body jerking and throbbing, his arms locking around me.

We shook together.

Shuddered together.

And when it was over, we stayed sweaty, breathless, tangled.

Whole.

It was everything.

Epilogue

ELIZA

Six months later…

It was the kind of day that made Briar Hill feel like a storybook.

Blue sky. Soft breeze. Not a single glitter spill in sight. We'd claimed a grassy corner of the park with too many blankets, three coolers, and enough Thorne sister energy to make the ducks rethink their life choices.

Clay was at the grill, flipping burgers with his usual quiet focus. Simon and Tanner were deep in a debate over charcoal versus gas, complete with historical references (Simon) and profanity (Tanner). Dean stood nearby, arms crossed, offering one word of input every five minutes, still winning the argument.

Veronica had already vetoed the disposable cutlery.

“I brought real forks,” she said, unfolding linen napkins like classified documents. “Because I have standards.”

“I brought wine,” said Vivian, lifting a bottle from a sequined tote. “Because I don’t.”

Lola rolled her eyes. “Where’s Eliza?”

“I’m here!” I called, holding up a canvas tote.

Three heads turned. Four, if you counted Dean’s subtle but very alert glance.

“That’s the surprise activity voice,” Vivian muttered. “I *hate* the surprise activity voice.”

I turned on my best Eliza smile and knelt beside the blanket, pulling out a stack of soft cotton t-shirts. “I made picnic shirts!”

All three of them groaned in unison.

“I swear,” Lola said, “if mine says something like *Sunshine Sister,* I’m drinking the citronella.”

“It doesn’t,” I promised, passing them out. “Just try them on.”

Veronica glanced down and smiled: *Best Aunt Ever.*

Lola unfolded hers next: *Promoted to Aunt.*

Vivian blinked at hers: *Aunt-in-Training.*

Three sets of eyes flicked to me in perfect unison.

I pulled out the last shirt—blush pink, folded with care: *Baby Thorne-Walker Coming Soon.*

Veronica gasped. Vivian screamed. Lola tackled me with a hug that nearly knocked the breath out of me.

"You're serious?" she whispered, already tearing up.

I nodded, barely able to speak. "We are."

Clay stepped up behind me, one hand settling gently over my stomach.

Veronica kissed my cheek. Vivian blinked hard and fanned her face. "Okay, well now I'm emotional *and* furious. Why didn't you give us a waterproof mascara warning?"

Lola swore under her breath and hugged me tighter.

And just when the noise began to settle, Vivian leaned back and looked at her shirt again.

"Wait," she sniffed. "Why does mine say *in training?*"

I shrugged. "Felt accurate."

Vivian turned to Veronica. "Yours doesn't say *in training.*"

Veronica just sipped her wine. "Doesn't need to."

Later, when the grill had cooled and the sun dipped behind the trees, I curled up beside Clay on the picnic blanket, full and flushed with too many emotions to name.

Tanner was helping Lola stake down their blanket after a gust of wind tried to take it out like a parachute—his expression all focus, hers all fire. Vivian had hijacked the Bluetooth speaker and was coaching Dean through a slow shimmy. He looked pained. She looked delighted. Veronica and Simon sat side by side on a quilt, pretending to read—but mostly stealing kisses when they thought no one was looking.

Clay laced his fingers with mine.

"You're glowing," he said softly.

I laughed. "Still?"

"Always."

I leaned my head on his shoulder, his heartbeat steady beneath my cheek.

And for the first time in a long time, I felt like every part of me, the sweet, the silly, the soft, was not just seen but celebrated.

***

Dear Reader,

Thank you so much for reading *Lessons & Leather*! I hope Eliza and Clay's story wrapped around your heart the same way it wrapped around mine—quietly at first, then all at once.

This book was a love letter to softness and strength, to unexpected chemistry, and to the kind of tenderness that makes you feel safe enough to fall apart—and bold enough to fall in love. Watching Eliza step into her own power, and Clay learn to believe he was worthy of hers, was one of the most emotional journeys I've written.

If their story made you smile, swoon, or even tear up just a little—I'd be so grateful if you left a review. Every single one helps readers find the Thorne Sisters and makes it possible for me to keep telling stories like this one. You can review the book on Amazon here.

Thank you for spending time in Briar Hill. And if you've read the whole Thorne Sisters series, I hope you know by now—whatever kind of woman you are, you are not too much. You are not not enough. You are just right.

With love,

Hana York

***

If you haven't met the rest of the Thorne sisters yet, now's the perfect time! Each book can be read as a standalone, but together they're a delicious journey through Briar Hill's boldest, fiercest, most unforgettable women. Find them all on Amazon!

Book One: *Ink & Iron*

A grumpy, guarded veteran. A tattoo artist who turns pain into beauty.

When trust feels like temptation, survival won't be enough.

Tanner Maddox didn't come to Briar Hill looking for second chances. He came to outrun the past, bury the guilt, and forget the wreckage he left behind. But one step into Needle & Ink—and one sharp-eyed artist who turns scars into stories—shatters every line he swore he wouldn't cross.

Lola Thorne knows better than to get tangled in someone else's broken pieces. She's got a tattoo shop to run, a past she won't talk about, and one rule she never breaks: don't fall for clients. Especially not a brooding ex-soldier with hands built for violence and a gaze that feels like a promise she can't afford to believe.

The tattoo was supposed to be just a cover. Instead, it uncovers the one thing neither of them thought they deserved: a future. He's all muscle, silence, and pain. She's all sharp edges, rough laughter, and a heart stitched together with ink and stubbornness. Together, they're something neither of them expected—and everything they didn't know how to want.

Walls will crumble. Rules will shatter. And when it's all stripped bare, the only thing left will be the truth—and the fight for a love worth every scar.

***Ink & Iron* is a steamy, emotional small-town romance about a grumpy veteran, a fierce tattoo artist, slow-burn tension, off-the-charts chemistry, and**

love so raw it leaves a mark deeper than skin.

***Ink & Iron* is available on Amazon here.**

Book Two: *Silk & Silence*

She's built her world on control. He's forgotten what it means to want. But some sparks don't ask permission before they burn.

Vivian Thorne built her life on polish, power, and impeccable control. As the owner of the Velvet Room—a high-end burlesque club known for its vintage glamours—she knows how to captivate a crowd without ever letting anyone close. Love is a liability she can't afford—and perfection is the armor she never removes.

Dean Thatcher is a gruff, guarded divorce attorney who's seen every way love can break, bleed, and betray. He doesn't do risks. He doesn't do chaos. And he sure as hell doesn't fall for women who look like trouble wrapped in red lipstick and secrets.

Their connection should have been a brief spark—an impulse easy to ignore. But the more Dean uncovers the woman beneath the polish, the more he realizes she's the most dangerously real thing he's ever craved. And the more Vivian lets him in, the more terrified she is that he'll walk away when he sees the cracks no amount of armor can hide.

Armor will crack. Hearts will break open. And when survival isn't enough anymore, they'll have to risk everything—for a love that strips them bare.

Silk & Silence is a steamy, emotional small-town romance about fierce vulnerability, slow-burn passion, and love without conditions. Perfect for fans of broken heroes, scarred heroines, emotional healing, and off-the-charts chemistry.

Silk & Silence **is available on Amazon here.**

Book Three: *Pleasure & Prose*

She's pure confidence and provocation. He's all restraint and repressed desire. But when opposites combust, even the rules don't stand a chance.

Simon Radcliffe is a buttoned-up British professor teaching at the local university, all nervous smiles and devastatingly proper manners. But when a wrong turn leads him through the doors of Pleasure & Co., he meets Veronica Thorne—a woman who exudes power, mystery, and the kind of sensual self-possession that makes him forget how to breathe.

Veronica doesn't do flustered. And she definitely doesn't go for repressed academics. But there's something about Simon—something curious and unguarded—that makes her pause. And when he asks her to tea—with the stiff sincerity of a man completely out of his depth—she says yes. Against every instinct, she says yes.

What begins as a slow, simmering pull becomes a wildfire neither of them is ready for. And when the past rears its nosy, unwelcome head, they'll have to decide what they're really fighting for.

Pleasure & Prose is a steamy, emotional small-town romance about opposites that ignite, slow burns that explode, and a cinnamon roll hero who learns the right woman doesn't just unravel you—she shows you who you've been all along.

Pleasure & Prose **is available on Amazon here.**

Hana York Books

Hearts on Duty Series

Sparks of Temptation

Love's Anchor

On Call for You

Investigating Desire

Falling for the Rescue

A Heart Worth Mending

***

Falling for the Billionaire Series

Hating Mr. Wentworth

Tempting Mr. Dawson

Unraveling Mr. Ashford

***

The Thorne Sisters Series

Ink & Iron

Silk & Silence

Pleasure & Prose

Lessons & Leather

***

The Men of Hawks Landing

Mountain Made

Mountain Found

Mountain Promise

Mountain Kept

***

For a full list of titles, please visit Hana York's website

www.HanaYork.com

About the Author

Hana York writes fast-paced, heart-pounding contemporary romance packed with irresistible heroes, strong heroines, laugh-out-loud banter, and just the right amount of spice to keep things sizzling. Her books are for readers who love grumpy men falling hard, fierce women who don't need saving, and the kind of chemistry that sparks off the page.

When she's not crafting stories full of love, tension, and toe-curling moments, you'll find her daydreaming about small-town charm, plotting ridiculous meet-cutes, and consuming an unhealthy amount of coffee. She believes in happily-ever-afters, overprotective heroes who don't stand a chance against their heroines, and that every great love story should come with a side of sass.

If you love forced proximity, off-limits attraction, sizzling tension, and romance that makes your heart race, welcome to the world of Hana York!

Follow Hana York for new releases, exclusive content, and behind-the-scenes fun! www.HanaYork.com

Find all her books here: https://www.amazon.com/author/hanayork

Follow her on Instagram: https://www.instagram.com/hanayorkromance/

Follow her on TikTok: https://www.tiktok.com/@hanayorkauthor

Follow her on Facebook: https://www.facebook.com/hanayorkromance/

Follow her on Good Reads: https://www.goodreads.com/author/show/54826946.Hana_York

Join her mailing list here: https://www.hanayork.com/subscribe

More to Read

If you enjoyed this story, I've got more where that came from! Keep reading for a look at my other books.

Hearts on Duty Series

Sparks of Temptation

A sizzling small-town romance where forced proximity turns up the heat between a stubborn chef and a protective firefighter.

Olivia Harper came to Anchor Bay for a fresh start—not a flirty distraction. After rebuilding her life, she has no time for complications, especially the kind that come with broad shoulders, a cocky grin, and a hero complex.

Jack Lawson knows how to keep his cool under pressure. As a firefighter, protecting people is second nature. But Olivia? She doesn't want rescuing, and she sure as hell doesn't want him getting too close. When a plumbing mishap lands him as her unexpected housemate, their battle of wills turns into something neither of them can ignore.

The problem? Olivia has spent years proving she doesn't need anyone, while Jack's instincts tell him to stand back before he wants something he can't have. But some flames refuse to die out...**A small town full of charm. A slow-burn romance packed with heat. A love story that proves the best things in life are worth the risk.**

***

Love's Anchor

A sizzling small-town romance where years of friendship ignite into something neither of them can ignore.

Brooke Taylor has spent years keeping her feelings for Theo Morgan buried beneath sharp comebacks and stubborn denial. As a no-nonsense cop in Anchor Bay, she's never let emotions get in the way of the job—especially when it comes to the charming, frustrating bar owner who knows exactly how to push her buttons.

Theo has always played it safe when it comes to Brooke. She's his best friend, his steady constant—the one woman he can't afford to lose. But when a break-in at his bar forces them into close quarters, the tension between them finally boils over.

Can they risk their friendship to take a chance on love? Or will fear keep them apart forever?**A small town full of charm. A slow-burn romance packed with heat. A love story where friendship is just the beginning.**

***

On Call for You

He swore she was off-limits. She's ready to prove him wrong.

Dr. Sophie Whitaker has spent her career proving herself in a world that underestimates her. As a brilliant but petite doctor, she's fought for respect every step of the way. Moving back to Anchor Bay is supposed to be a fresh start—not a temptation in the form of Lucas Carter. The rugged EMT with a cocky grin and a hero complex. The man her brother trusts with his life... and the one she should definitely stay away from.

Lucas Carter lives by two rules: stay cool under pressure and never, ever cross the line with Sophie Whitaker. Even if she's gorgeous. Even if she's sharp-witted and impossible to ignore. Even if, after one stormy encounter stranded together, the idea of walking away feels damn near impossible.

Now, every stolen glance and lingering touch has Lucas questioning everything—especially the rule that's kept him from going after the one woman he can't stop thinking about. Falling for Sophie could mean risking his oldest friendship. But walking away? That might be the biggest mistake of his life.

A sizzling, forbidden love, best friend's little sister romance packed with tension, heat, and undeniable chemistry!

***

Investigating Desire

A Slow-Burn Romantic Suspense with a Grumpy Detective and the Journalist Who Won't Back Down

Detective Nate Whitaker has sworn off love. After a messy divorce, he's buried himself in his work, content to keep his emotions locked away. But when a bold, relentless journalist starts shadowing him for an exclusive story, their push-and-pull dynamic ignites a slow burn neither of them can ignore.

Tessa Donovan has worked hard to make a name for herself. She's determined to crack open a case that's rocked this small town, even if it means getting under the skin of a brooding detective who wants nothing to do with her. But when her investigation stirs up danger, Nate has no choice but to keep her close. What starts as a reluctant partnership turns into something far more dangerous—a fiery attraction neither of them is ready for.

With a growing threat looming and tension crackling between them, this small-town romantic suspense is about to heat up. Can Nate and Tessa untangle the case before it's too late, or will their undeniable chemistry turn into the biggest risk of all?

***

Falling for the Rescue

A Forced Proximity, Search and Rescue Romance Packed with Heat, Heart, and High Stakes

Ryan Anderson thrives in the chaos of Search and Rescue, risking everything to save those in danger. He's fiercely independent, highly skilled, and never the one needing help—until a treacherous storm and a botched rescue mission leave him stranded, injured, and facing the one situation he can't control.

Enter Sam Monroe—a tough, no-nonsense ex-military K9 handler who's spent years proving she doesn't need anyone. Haunted by her past and more comfortable in survival mode than emotional entanglements, Sam doesn't have time for distractions—especially not the kind with broad shoulders, smoldering intensity, and a stubborn streak to match her own.

Forced to wait out the storm in a remote cabin in the wilderness, their reluctant alliance turns into something far more dangerous. Tensions ignite. Sparks fly. But neither of them is built for surrender—especially when old wounds and hidden vulnerabilities threaten to unravel the fragile trust between them.

Will Sam and Ryan let down their walls and take a risk on love? Or will fear and pride keep them from the one person who finally sees them for who they truly are?

***

A Heart Worth Mending

Penelope Everett is chaos wrapped in sunshine and cinnamon. Milo Turner is a brooding small-town vet who prefers his solitude—and his scars—untouched.

But when an injured fox, a runaway goat, and a perfectly imperfect dance in a flour-dusted kitchen spark something real, Milo and Penelope are forced to face the truth: love isn't always neat. It's messy. It's brave. It's terrifying.

And sometimes... it's exactly what you need to heal.

Can a woman learning to choose herself risk everything on a man still learning how to stay?**A Heart Worth Mending is a small-town, age-gap romance packed with heart, heat, and a hero worth waiting for. Perfect for fans of grumpy-sunshine pairings, emotionally satisfying slow burns, and heroines who never stop believing in love—even when it hurts.**

***

***

Falling for the Billionaire Series

Hating Mr. Wentworth

They're supposed to be enemies—so why does arguing feel like foreplay?

Liz Bentley built her career on grit, caffeine, and a zero-tolerance policy for entitled men—especially not the newly appointed CEO with a famous last name and a face straight off a magazine cover. Brett Wentworth might be rich, polished, and maddeningly smug, but Liz knows his type: privilege, power, and betrayal wrapped in a designer suit.

Brett didn't ask to inherit the mess his father made of Bright Spark. But the moment Liz storms into his boardroom—all fire, wit, and defiance—he knows two things: she's the sharpest mind in the company... and the one woman he shouldn't want.

Their arguments are electric. Their chemistry, impossible to ignore. And one dangerously hot encounter changes everything. Now Brett has one shot to prove he's nothing like the men who came before—and everything Liz never saw coming.

Enemies on paper. Fireworks in person. A hot, hilarious romance that's one HR violation away from disaster—or the most delicious kind of downfall.

***

Tempting Mr. Dawson

A sizzling, laugh-out-loud billionaire romcom about mistaken identity, forbidden chemistry, and the hidden moment that might just lead to love.

Travel writer Piper Winslow is in paradise—but she's not here to relax. Her assignment? Review Coral Bay Resort and keep things strictly professional. But the guy in the Hawaiian shirt who offers her a "real" tour of the property? He's messing with her objectivity—and tempting her to break all her rules.

Logan Dawson didn't mean to lie. When Piper mistakes him for a charming staff member instead of the CEO of the luxury resort she's reviewing, he doesn't correct her. For once, someone sees him, not his title. And walking away from that? Not so easy.

What starts as playful banter turns into an afternoon of unforgettable heat in a hidden grotto. But when the truth comes out, so does the fallout. Now Logan has to prove that the man she fell for is the real him—and that what sparked between them wasn't just a vacation fling.

Tempting Mr. Dawson is a steamy billionaire romcom with sharp banter, tropical heat, mistaken identities, and a CEO who'll risk everything to win back the woman who saw through him.

***

Unraveling Mr. Ashford

Mia Wilder is a glitter bomb of chaos, creativity, and caffeine—and even she knows it's time for a vacation when her vision board catches fire. (Literally.)

So when a family friend pulls strings to score her a solo escape to a luxury island resort, Mia says yes—because nothing says self-care like seven days of sunshine, silence, and SPF 50.

Thanks to a booking snafu—and a storm that knocks out all communication—Mia finds herself stranded with Grant Ashford, a brooding tech billionaire who clearly didn't plan on sharing his R&R with an overcaffeinated sunbeam who narrates her inner monologue like it's a podcast.

He's grumpy, guarded, and allergic to distractions. She's sunshine in designer flip-flops. And neither of them is prepared for what happens next.

***

***

The Thorne Sisters Series

Ink & Iron

A grumpy, guarded veteran. A tattoo artist who turns pain into beauty. When trust feels like temptation, survival won't be enough.

Tanner Maddox didn't come to Briar Hill looking for second chances. He came to outrun the past, bury the guilt, and forget the wreckage he left behind. But one step into Needle & Ink—and one sharp-eyed artist who turns scars into stories—shatters every line he swore he wouldn't cross.

Lola Thorne knows better than to get tangled in someone else's broken pieces. She's got a tattoo shop to run, a past she won't talk about, and one rule she never breaks: don't fall for clients. Especially not a brooding ex-soldier with hands built for violence and a gaze that feels like a promise she can't afford to believe.

The tattoo was supposed to be just a cover. Instead, it uncovers the one thing neither of them thought they deserved: a future. He's all muscle, silence, and pain. She's all sharp edges, rough laughter, and a heart stitched together with ink and stubbornness. Together, they're something neither of them expected—and everything they didn't know how to want.

Walls will crumble. Rules will shatter. And when it's all stripped bare, the only thing left will be the truth—and the fight for a love worth every scar.

Ink & Iron is a steamy, emotional small-town romance about a grumpy veteran, a fierce tattoo artist, slow-burn tension, off-the-charts chemistry, and love so raw it leaves a mark deeper than skin.

***

Silk & Silence

She's built her world on control. He's forgotten what it means to want. But some sparks don't ask permission before they burn.

Vivian Thorne built her life on polish, power, and impeccable control. As the owner of the Velvet Room—a high-end burlesque club known for its vintage glamours—she knows how to captivate a crowd without ever letting anyone close. Love is a liability she can't afford—and perfection is the armor she never removes.

Dean Thatcher is a gruff, guarded divorce attorney who's seen every way love can break, bleed, and betray. He doesn't do risks. He doesn't do chaos. And he sure as hell doesn't fall for women who look like trouble wrapped in red lipstick and secrets.

Their connection should have been a brief spark—an impulse easy to ignore. But the more Dean uncovers the woman beneath the polish, the more he realizes she's the most dangerously real thing he's ever craved. And the more Vivian lets him in, the more terrified she is that he'll walk away when he sees the cracks no amount of armor can hide.Masks will slip. Hearts will break open. And when survival isn't enough anymore, they'll have to risk everything—for a love that strips them bare.

Silk & Silence is a steamy, emotional small-town romance about fierce vulnerability, slow-burn passion, and love without conditions. Perfect for fans of broken heroes, scarred heroines, emotional healing, and off-the-charts chemistry.

***

Pleasure & Prose

She's pure confidence and provocation. He's all restraint and repressed desire. But when opposites combust, even the rules don't stand a chance.

Simon Radcliffe is a buttoned-up British professor teaching at the local university, all nervous smiles and devastatingly proper manners. But when a wrong turn leads him through the doors of Pleasure & Co., he meets Veronica Thorne—a woman who exudes power, mystery, and the kind of sensual self-possession that makes him forget how to breathe.

Veronica doesn't do flustered. And she definitely doesn't go for repressed academics. But there's something about Simon—something curious and unguarded—that makes her pause. And when he asks her to tea—with the stiff sincerity of a man completely out of his depth—she says yes. Against every instinct, she says yes.

What begins as a slow, simmering pull becomes a wildfire neither of them is ready for. And when the past rears its nosy, unwelcome head, they'll have to decide what they're really fighting for.

Pleasure & Prose is a steamy, emotional small-town romance about opposites that ignite, slow burns that explode, and a cinnamon roll hero who learns the right woman doesn't just unravel you—she shows you who you've been all along.

***

Lessons & Leather

She's never been touched. He's never been trusted. But when a sunshine schoolteacher crashes into a broody mechanic—literally—the sparks don't stop flying.

Eliza Thorne has spent her whole life being good. Good daughter. Good sister. Good teacher. She keeps the peace, keeps things running, and keeps her deepest desires tucked safely out of sight. Wanting more has never felt like an option—until a fender bender introduces her to Clay Walker, the town's broodiest mechanic with a jaw that could cut glass and eyes that see far too much.

Clay doesn't do soft. Doesn't do complications. He keeps his head down, runs his garage, and avoids anything that might crack the armor he's spent years building. But Eliza Thorne—sunshine smile, cherry earrings, and quiet strength—doesn't just crack his walls. She dismantles them.

Their connection is electric. Impossible. Inevitable. But if they want more than just heat, they'll have to believe something neither of them has ever been told—that real love doesn't just hold space—it makes you feel like you belong in it.

Lessons & Leather is a steamy, small-town opposites-attract romance between a woman learning to

want and a man learning he's wanted. Featuring emotional firsts, protective tension, and the kind of slow burn that scorches when it finally ignites

***

***

The Men of Hawks Landing Series

Mountain Made

She came to the mountain to say goodbye. He was never part of the plan.

Anastasia Blake isn't running—at least, not in the way people think. The mountain cabin her grandmother left her was meant to be a quick project. Fix it. Sell it. Move on. But the moment she steps through the door, memories stir—of laughter, freedom, and the girl she used to be before the world told her who to become.

Travis Holt doesn't do drama, and he definitely doesn't do complications. But Anastasia? She's all sunlight and sharp edges, and she sees straight through the walls he's spent years perfecting. He's supposed to be there to help her leave—but the longer she stays, the harder it is to imagine letting her go. It was supposed to be easy. One moment. One goodbye. But some goodbyes aren't meant to be.

Mountain Made is a steamy, slow-burn romance about opposites who were never meant to attract, forced proximity that turns into something real, emotional healing, and a sexy mountain man who falls first and never looks back.

***

Mountain Found

Leaving the altar was the only decision she could make. Finding safety in the town's broodiest mechanic? That felt like fate.

Cal Mason wasn't looking for trouble. But trouble just took the room above his garage. Grace Sinclair didn't plan to become a runaway bride. But when forever with the wrong man became unbearable, she walked out mid-ceremony and kept driving until the mountains stopped her. Hawk's Landing was supposed to be a place to catch her breath—not to fall into the arms of a broody mechanic with hands that know how to rebuild broken things.

Cal Mason has no interest in complications. And Grace? She's nothing but complicated. Too polished. Too stubborn. Way too tempting. But when her past shows up at his door, Cal does what he's always done—protects what's his.

Her past wants her back. But Cal's already claimed her future.

Mountain Found is a steamy, emotional small-town romance about a runaway bride, a broody mechanic with a mile-wide protective streak, undeniable chemistry, and a love strong enough to stand against the past.

***

Mountain Promise

They were supposed to fake forever. Until he made her want the real thing.

Rowan McClaren has a plan: save her mother's legacy, keep the animal hospital running, and avoid needing anyone—especially a man. But when a legal loophole puts everything at risk, there's only one option left: marry someone. Fast.

Enter Miles Griffin—grumpy ex-soldier, resident plumber at Hawk's Landing Lodge, and the last person

looking for a relationship. But when Rowan's quiet desperation meets Miles's steady
loyalty, they strike a deal: one marriage. One shared roof. No feelings.

It's supposed to be simple. But the longer Miles shares her space—the more he fixes what's broken and holds her like he means it—the harder it gets to remember what's fake. Because falling for Miles Griffin wasn't part of the deal. But it might be the only thing that makes sense now.

Mountain Promise is a steamy, slow-burn small-town romance about a grumpy ex-soldier, a fiercely independent heroine, one fake "I do," and the real love they never saw coming.

***

Mountain Kept

She's his best friend's little sister—vibrant, fearless,and completely off-limits. He's the town flirt who's never let anyone close...until her.

Lucy Griffin is tired of being the afterthought. Bold and full of life, she wants more than surface-level affection—she wants something real. And the only person who's ever made her feel truly seen? The one man she's never supposed to want.

Eli Granger hides behind charm and easy grins. He doesn't do complicated. Doesn't do commitment. And definitely doesn't mess around with Miles Griffin's little sister. But when Lucy shows up in Hawk's Landing and turns his carefully curated life upside down, every rule starts to crack.

Then a storm leaves them stranded together in the woods—and one night changes everything.

She wants to be chosen. He's terrified to want anything real. And falling for her could cost him the only family he's ever known.

A steamy, small-town best friend's sister romance with forbidden tension, slow-burn heat, and a flirty hero who finally meets his match.

***

To stay up to date on all of my releases, subscribe to my mailing list here!

www.ingramcontent.com/pod-product-compliance
Lightning Source LLC
Chambersburg PA
CBHW072231190626
46809CB00017B/1702
9781967053346